D1567080

FACING LIFE'S CHALLENGES

FACING DEATH

BY STEPHANIE FINNE

BLUE OWL
BOOKS

TIPS FOR CAREGIVERS

Social and emotional learning (SEL) helps children manage emotions, create and achieve goals, maintain relationships, learn how to feel empathy, and make good decisions. The SEL approach will help children establish positive habits in communication, cooperation, and decision-making. By incorporating SEL in early reading, children will be better equipped to build confidence and foster positive peer networks.

BEFORE READING

Talk to the reader about death. Explain that everyone grieves the loss of a loved one differently.

Discuss: What does death mean to you? How do you feel when someone you love is gone? Can you name the different emotions?

AFTER READING

Talk to the reader about the different stages of grief.

Discuss: What emotions do you feel when someone you love dies? How do you work through them?

SEL GOAL

Some students may struggle with sadness related to the death of a loved one. Help readers develop a vocabulary to voice their feelings. Help them learn to stop and think about their emotions and how to process them. Have students divide into small groups. Within their groups, have them talk about different emotions. Have any of them dealt with the loss of a loved one? What emotions did they feel? What did they do to feel better?

TABLE OF CONTENTS

CHAPTER 1

LOSING A LOVED ONE

Logan's mom has sad news. Logan's grandpa has died. Logan feels very sad and confused. He talks with his mom about his **emotions**.

Death is the ending of life. Everyone will die one day. At some point, you may lose someone you love. It could be a grandparent, parent, or friend. Death is incredibly sad. But there are healthy ways to **cope**.

CHAPTER 2

THE GRIEVING PROCESS

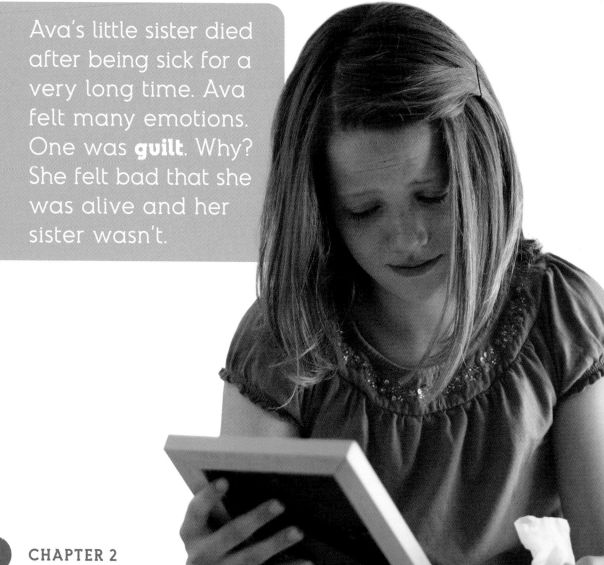

Ava's little sister died after being sick for a very long time. Ava felt many emotions. One was **guilt**. Why? She felt bad that she was alive and her sister wasn't.

Not everyone **reacts** to death the same way. When Zack's mom dies, he is scared. What will the future be like? Will someone else die? His dad helps. He lets Zack know he is always there for him.

Many people feel **grief**. This is deep sadness. Everyone grieves differently. Some people cry. Others are quiet.

There are stages of grief. Everyone experiences them differently. One is having a hard time **accepting** the death. Another is anger. Some even become **depressed**.

Sometimes we feel grief before someone dies. Sam's mom is **terminally ill**. She knows she will lose her. She feels the grief beforehand.

She and her mother take pictures together. They celebrate the things they love doing with each other. Sam's mother even writes her a letter. After she is gone, Sam can read it to remember her mom.

After someone dies, it helps to **identify** and **process** your emotions. How can you do this? Try writing a poem. Or write in a journal. Drawing helps Malcolm process.

You can talk to a loved one. It may be difficult. But talking about your feelings will help. You are not alone in your grief. The people who love you want to help you feel better. They may be feeling the same way.

HAPPY MEMORIES

Sharing memories can help you process your emotions. You can talk about the person. Or you can look at pictures. This helps keep good memories alive.

After someone dies, people may attend a **funeral**. At a funeral, people gather to say goodbye. There may be praying and music. It is a good time to share stories about the loved one. There are a lot of emotions at a funeral.

WAYS TO HONOR DEATH

A funeral is not the only way to honor a death. Wakes happen before funerals. A memorial may take place at a person's home or at a school. A celebration of life is a casual, more upbeat gathering.

funeral

CHAPTER 3

HELPING OTHERS GRIEVE

Eli's friend has died. James isn't quite sure what to do. But he wants to **comfort** Eli. He tells Eli he is sorry for his loss. He listens to Eli talk about his feelings.

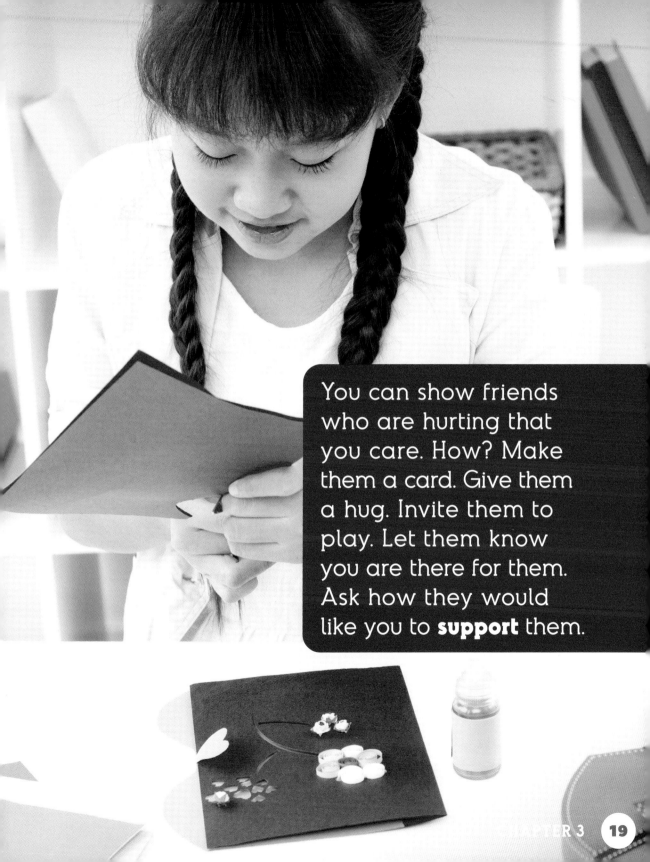

You can show friends who are hurting that you care. How? Make them a card. Give them a hug. Invite them to play. Let them know you are there for them. Ask how they would like you to **support** them.

You won't always be able to help. If you are worried about your friend, talk to an adult. An adult can help support your friend.

Death is hard for everyone. It is important to identify your feelings and talk to your friends and family about them. With time, you will feel better.

CHANGING BEHAVIOR

Your friend may act differently after a loved one dies. They may be quiet or angry. It won't last forever. Keep being their friend. Let them know you are there for them.

GOALS AND TOOLS

GROW WITH GOALS

Death is a difficult thing to process. Here are a few things you can try after someone has died.

Goal: Think about what you are feeling. Name the emotions as you experience them. You may feel angry, sad, guilty, or scared.

Goal: Talk to a friend or adult about what you are feeling. You are not alone. It helps to know that other people experience many of the same emotions.

Goal: Start a journal. Draw or write how you are feeling each day. Fill the journal with memories of your loved one.

MINDFULNESS EXERCISE

When you are feeling overwhelmed or need to take a moment, practicing mindfulness and breathing can help.

- Make a fist with each hand.

- Take a deep breath in.

- As you exhale, uncurl one finger. Start with the thumb of one hand.

- Pause and inhale.

- For each breath, uncurl another finger.

- Continue until you have both palms open in your lap.

GLOSSARY

accepting
Agreeing that something is correct, satisfactory, or enough.

comfort
To calm or reassure someone.

cope
To deal with something effectively.

depressed
Having a medical condition in which you feel unhappy or hopeless and can't concentrate or sleep well.

emotions
Feelings, such as happiness, sadness, or anger.

funeral
A memorial ceremony that happens shortly after a death and often includes a burial.

grief
A feeling of great sadness or deep distress.

guilt
A feeling of shame for thinking you have done something wrong.

identify
To recognize what something is.

process
To gain an understanding or acceptance of something.

reacts
Behaves in a particular way as a response to things that have happened.

support
To give help, comfort, or encouragement to someone or something.

terminally ill
Having an illness that cannot be cured and will lead to death.

TO LEARN MORE

FACT SURFER

Finding more information is as easy as 1, 2, 3.

1. Go to www.factsurfer.com

2. Enter "**facingdeath**" into the search box.

3. Choose your cover to see a list of websites.

INDEX

Blue Owl Books are published by Jump!, 5357 Penn Avenue South, Minneapolis, MN 55419, www.jumplibrary.com

Library of Congress Cataloging-in-Publication Data

Names: Finne, Stephanie, author.
Title: Facing death / Stephanie Finne.
Description: Minneapolis: Jump!, Inc., 2021.
Series: Facing life's challenges | Includes index.
Audience: Ages 7–10 | Audience: Grades 2–3
Identifiers: LCCN 2019055132 (print)
LCCN 2019055133 (ebook)
ISBN 9781645274100 (hardcover)
ISBN 9781645274117 (paperback)
ISBN 9781645274124 (ebook)
Subjects: LCSH: Grief—Juvenile literature. | Loss (Psychology)—Juvenile literature.
Children—Death—Psychological aspects—Juvenile literature.
Classification: LCC BF575.G7 F5546 2021 (print) | LCC BF575.G7 (ebook) | DDC 155.9/37—dc23
LC record available at https://lccn.loc.gov/2019055132
LC ebook record available at https://lccn.loc.gov/2019055133

Editor: Jenna Gleisner
Designer: Jenna Casura

Photo Credits: RubberBall Productions/Getty, cover, 16–17; Diego Cervo/Shutterstock, 1 (image); Hanzi-mor/Shutterstock, 1 (frame); CREATISTA/Shutterstock, 3; Brastock/
Shutterstock, 4; lisafx/iStock, 5; Mike Kemp/Getty, 6; Motortion/iStock, 7, 18; Photoroyalty/Shutterstock, 8–9; Dean Drobot/Shutterstock, 10–11; Wavebreak Media ltd/Alamy,
12–13; shironosov/iStock, 14–15; Dragon Images/Shutterstock, 19; Lopolo/Shutterstock, 20–21.

Printed in the United States of America at Corporate Graphics in North Mankato, Minnesota.